Here's what kids and grown-ups have to say about the Magic Tree House® books:

"Oh, man . . . the Magic Tree House series
is really exciting!"
—Christina

"I like the Magic Tree House series. I stay up
all night reading them. Even on school nights!"
—Peter

"Jack and Annie have opened a door to a world
of literacy that I know will continue throughout
the lives of my students."
—Deborah H.

"As a librarian, I have seen many happy young
readers coming into the library to check out
the next Magic Tree House book in the series."
—Lynne H.

Magic Tree House® Merlin Missions

For a list of all the Magic Tree House® titles,
visit MagicTreeHouse.com.

MAGIC TREE HOUSE®
MERLIN MISSIONS

#2 HAUNTED CASTLE ON HALLOWS EVE

BY MARY POPE OSBORNE
ILLUSTRATED BY SAL MURDOCCA

A STEPPING STONE BOOK™
Random House 🏠 New York

For Will, the <u>real</u> magician
in the heart of the oak

Text copyright © 2003 by Mary Pope Osborne
Cover art and interior illustrations copyright © 2003 by Sal Murdocca

Visit us on the Web!
MagicTreeHouse.com

Educators and librarians, for a variety of teaching tools, visit us at
RHTeachersLibrarians.com

The Library of Congress has cataloged the hardcover edition of this work as follows:
Osborne, Mary Pope.
Haunted castle on Hallows Eve / by Mary Pope Osborne ; illustrated by Sal Murdocca.
   p.   cm. — (Magic tree house ; #30)
"A Stepping Stone book."
Summary: In their magic treehouse, Jack and Annie are again transported to King Arthur's realm, where invisible beings, giant ravens, and mistaken magic spells have a duke's castle in an uproar on Halloween night.
ISBN 978-0-375-82521-7 (trade) — ISBN 978-0-375-92521-4 (lib. bdg.) —
ISBN 978-0-307-53064-6 (ebook)
[1. Haunted houses—Fiction. 2. Castles—Fiction. 3. Ravens—Fiction.
4. Halloween—Fiction. 5. Time travel—Fiction. 6. Magic—Fiction.
7. Tree houses—Fiction.] I. Murdocca, Sal, ill. II. Title.
PZ7.O81167Hat 2003 [Fic]—dc21 2002156313

ISBN 978-0-375-86090-4 (pbk.)

Printed in the United States of America
23 22 21 20 19 18

This book has been officially leveled by using the F&P Text Level Gradient™
Leveling System.

CONTENTS

Dear Reader,

Haunted Castle on Hallows Eve is the second in a special group of Magic Tree House books called "The Merlin Missions." In these books, it is Merlin the magician who sends Jack and Annie on their tree house adventures, often to mythical and legendary lands.

In the first Merlin Mission, Christmas in Camelot, Jack and Annie journeyed into a world of magic and fantasy to find a secret cauldron that held the Water of Memory and Imagination.

Now, nearly a year later, Jack and Annie are about to set out on a new Merlin Mission. They invite you to come with them to an outlying realm of Camelot where strange and eerie things are happening at a duke's castle.

Enjoy your journey! But beware—in the world of Merlin the magician, <u>anything</u> can happen. . . .

Mary Pope Osborne

The hearth is cold in the lonely hall,
No banquet decks the board;
No page stands ready at the call,
To 'tend his wearied lord.

From "Earl Desmond and the Banshee"
—Anonymous

CHAPTER ONE

All Hallows Eve

"Maybe I should be a vampire instead of a princess," said Annie.

She and Jack were sitting on their front porch. A cool breeze rustled the trees. Autumn leaves twirled to the ground.

"But you already have your princess costume," said Jack. "Besides, you were a vampire last Halloween."

"I know, but I want to wear my big teeth again," said Annie.

"So wear your big teeth and be a vampire-princess," said Jack. He stood up. "I'm going to go put on my ghoul makeup now."

KRAW!

"Oh, man!" said Jack.

A giant black bird swooped down to the ground. The bird strutted through the fallen leaves. Its feathers glistened in the golden afternoon light.

"Wow, is that a crow?" asked Annie.

"It's too big for a crow," said Jack. "I think it might be a raven."

"A *raven*?" said Annie. "Cool."

The raven lifted its sleek head and stared at them with bright eyes. Jack held his breath.

The bird hopped forward. It flapped its great black wings and lifted into the air. Then he glided into the autumn sky and headed toward the Frog Creek woods.

Annie jumped up. "It's a sign! Morgan's back!" she said.

"I think you're right!" said Jack. "Let's go!"

Jack and Annie hurried across their front yard, crunching through the leaves. They ran up their street and into the Frog Creek woods.

When they came to the tallest oak, they saw the rope ladder swaying in the wind. The magic tree house was waiting for them.

"Just as we thought," Annie said, smiling.

Jack followed her up the ladder. When they climbed inside the tree house, they saw no sign of Morgan le Fay, the enchantress from the kingdom of Camelot.

"That's weird," said Jack, looking around.

The wind blew hard again, shaking the tree branches. A huge yellow leaf fluttered through the open window and came to rest at Jack's feet.

"Oh, man," he said. "Look at this."

"What?" said Annie.

Jack picked up the leaf. There was writing on it. The letters were curvy and old-fashioned.

"Wow," whispered Annie. "What does it say?"

Jack held the leaf up to the tree house

window. In the fading light, he read aloud:

To Jack and Annie of Frog Creek,
On All Hallows Eve,
look for me
in the heart of the oak.
—M.

"*M!*" said Annie. "Morgan never signs her messages with *M. . . .*"

"Right . . . ," said Jack. "But . . ."

"*Merlin* does!" they said together.

"Like when he sent us the invitation to spend Christmas in Camelot," said Annie. She pointed to the Royal Invitation that still lay in the corner of the tree house.

"Now he's inviting us on Halloween!" said

Jack. "Halloween was called 'All Hallows Eve' a long time ago."

"I know," said Annie. "We have to go!"

"Of course," said Jack. There was no way they could turn down an invitation from the master magician of all time. "But how do we get there?"

"I'll bet our invitation will take us," said Annie, "like when we went to King Arthur's castle on Christmas Eve."

"Good idea," said Jack. He pointed to the fancy writing on the leaf. "I wish we could go—uh—"

"To where this leaf invitation came from!" said Annie.

"Right!" said Jack.

The wind began to blow.

The tree house started to spin.

It spun faster and faster.

Then everything was still.

Absolutely still.

CHAPTER TWO

The Heart of the Oak

Jack opened his eyes. A chilly wind blew into the tree house. Oak leaves swirled outside the window.

"Look, we have our costumes," said Annie. "I'm not a princess *or* a vampire."

Jack looked at their clothes. He was wearing a knee-length tunic and tights. Annie was wearing a long dress with an apron.

"Camelot costumes," Jack said softly.

They looked out the window together. They were high in a huge oak tree in a thick forest.

The afternoon sun was low in the autumn sky.

"So what do we do now?" said Jack.

"The invitation says we're supposed to meet Merlin in the heart of the oak," said Annie.

"Yeah, but what does that mean?" said Jack, scowling. "The heart of an oak?"

"Let's go down and try to figure it out," said Annie.

She carefully placed their invitation in a corner of the tree house. Then she and Jack climbed down the rope ladder. They stepped onto the leafy ground. In the fading daylight, they began circling the base of the giant oak.

They walked all the way around, until they came to the rope ladder again.

"We're back where we started," said Jack. "We never found the heart."

"Wait a minute," said Annie. "What's that?" She pointed to a long, thin crack in the bark of the tree trunk. A sliver of light seemed to be coming from the crack.

Jack touched the bark around the light. He pushed. The crack got bigger.

"It's a secret door!" said Jack. He pushed harder. *Creak*. A tall, narrow door swung into the tree. Light streamed from inside.

"We found it," whispered Annie, "the heart of the oak."

Jack nodded.

"Let's go in," said Annie. They slipped through the narrow doorway into the bright hollow of the tree trunk.

Jack couldn't believe his eyes. The round room was lit with hundreds of candles. Shadows danced on the curved brown walls.

This isn't possible! thought Jack. The heart of the oak seemed much bigger than the tree itself!

"Welcome," said a deep, whispery voice.

They turned around and saw an old man sitting in a carved wooden chair. He had a long white beard and wore a red cloak.

"Hi, Merlin," said Annie.

"Hello, Annie. Hello, Jack. It is good to see you again," the magician said. "I am grateful for the help you gave us on Christmas Eve in Camelot. Now Morgan and I believe you might be able to help us again."

"We'd love to!" said Annie.

"The whole future of our kingdom depends upon your success," said Merlin.

"Are you sure you want *us*?" Jack asked. "I mean, we're just kids."

"You have passed many tests for Morgan," said Merlin. "Are you not Master Librarians and Magicians of Everyday Magic?"

Jack nodded. "Yes, we are," he said.

"Good. You will need all your skills on this mission," said Merlin. "You will also need a helper and guide from *our* world, the world of magic and legend."

"Are you coming with us?" asked Annie.

"No," the magician said. "Your guide shall be one much younger than I. He is in my library now. Yesterday he brought me some books I had requested from Morgan's library."

Merlin rose from his chair. "Come," he said, leading them to a door in the curved wall. He opened it and stepped into another room. Jack and Annie followed him.

The musty room was filled with scrolls and ancient-looking books. Sitting on the floor was a boy about eleven or twelve years old. He was reading by the light of a lantern.

"Your helper and guide," Merlin said to Jack and Annie.

The boy looked up. He had a friendly, freckled face and dark, twinkly eyes. He broke into a big grin.

"Arf, arf!" he said.

"Teddy!" cried Annie.

Jack couldn't believe it! Their helper was the young sorcerer who was training as Morgan's apprentice!

Merlin, for once, looked surprised. "You already know each other?" he asked.

"Yes, we met a while ago when I accidentally changed myself into a dog!" said Teddy.

"Morgan wanted to teach Teddy a lesson," explained Annie. "So she sent him with us on four tree-house journeys before she changed him back into a boy. He saved us on the *Titanic*. And he saved us from a buffalo stampede!"

"And from a tiger in India," said Jack, "and a forest fire in Australia."

"Wondrous journeys, indeed," said Merlin. "I am glad you are already friends. Your friendship may help you on this mission."

"What *is* our mission?" asked Annie.

"We are now in one of the outlying realms of Camelot," said Merlin. "Beyond these woods lies the castle of a duke."

Merlin leaned forward, as if he were about to tell them something really scary. "It will be your mission," he said, "to bring order to the duke's castle."

Merlin sat back in his chair. His gaze was calm, but a fierce light shone in his eyes.

Bring order to a castle? thought Jack. *Is that all?*

"Who messed it up, sir?" asked Annie.

"You will find out soon enough," said Merlin.

"We accept our assignment gladly," said Teddy. "The mission will be done without fail!"

Merlin fixed his gaze on Teddy. "Perhaps," he said. "But a warning, my boy: you are hasty and careless with your magic rhymes. On this mission, you must choose *all* your words wisely."

"Indeed I will," said Teddy.

Merlin turned to Jack and Annie. "And a warning to you, too," he said. "You are about to enter a tunnel of fear. Proceed onward with courage, and you will come out into the light."

Tunnel of fear? Jack thought.

Merlin picked up the lantern and handed it to Teddy. "The duke's castle lies to the east. Go quickly," he said. "Order must be restored as soon as possible."

Teddy nodded at Merlin. Then he turned to Jack and Annie. "To the duke's castle!" he said, and he led them out of the heart of the oak.

CHAPTER THREE

Rok

It was cooler outside now. Daylight was fading quickly. The wind had picked up.

"A grand adventure for us, eh?" said Teddy.

"Yes!" said Annie.

Jack was excited, too, but he had lots of questions. As Teddy started off through the oak forest, Jack hurried to keep up.

"What do you think our mission *is* exactly?" he asked.

"Merlin said we should bring order to the castle," said Annie.

"Perhaps he wants us to mop the floors and wash the dishes," Teddy joked.

"And make the beds!" said Annie. She and Teddy laughed.

"Our mission has to be harder than just doing chores," said Jack. "What about the tunnel of fear?"

"Oh, you need not be afraid of fear," said Teddy. "I know magic, remember?"

"Teddy, did you know any magic before you met Morgan and Merlin?" asked Annie.

"Ah, indeed. My father was a sorcerer," Teddy said. "And my mother was a wood sprite from the Otherworld."

"That is so cool," said Annie.

They crunched through piles of dead leaves. A gust of wind shook the tree branches. Golden oak leaves spun to the ground.

Jack's thoughts were spinning, too. Merlin in the heart of the oak, sorcerers, wood sprites—none of these things would ever make sense back in Frog Creek.

At last Teddy led them out of the forest and into a clearing. "Halt!" he said.

They all stopped walking. Beyond the clearing was a small village of thatched-roof cottages. The cottage windows twinkled with candlelight. Chimney smoke rose into the dusky sky.

Teddy held up his lantern. "Onward!" he said.

They went down a dirt path that passed through the village. Several children in ragged clothes peeked out their front doors.

"Greetings!" called Teddy. "Can you tell us how to get to the castle of the duke?"

"The castle?" a boy said in a frightened voice. "'Tis just beyond the wood!" He pointed at a forest on the other side of the village. "Follow the path and you'll come to it!"

"Oh, but you mustn't go there!" a girl cried.

"Why not?" asked Annie.

"Something's been very wrong at the castle," said the girl. "Ever since the ravens came!"

"Has anyone been there to see what's going on?" asked Jack.

"Only old Maggie, who used to work there," said the girl. "Two weeks ago, she went to the castle as usual. But she came running back, scared out of her wits."

"Maggie says the castle is all haunted with ghosts," said a boy. "She keeps repeating the same rhyme over and over."

"Ghosts?" said Jack. His mouth felt dry.

But Teddy just laughed. "Ghosts don't scare me!" he said.

"Have you ever seen one, Teddy?" asked Annie.

"No! But I should like to!" Teddy said with a grin.

"Look!" One of the girls pointed at the sky. "The ravens are back!"

A flock of large black birds was flying low in the dark gray sky. The village kids screamed. Several grown-ups rushed out of their cottages.

"Go away!" a woman yelled at the ravens. She picked up a handful of stones and began throwing them at the birds. "Leave us alone!"

"Stop! Stop!" cried Annie. "You'll hurt them!"

A stone struck one of the ravens. It fell to the ground.

"Oh, no!" cried Annie.

The grown-ups pulled their children inside. Doors slammed and shutters closed.

Annie dashed to the fallen bird and knelt beside it.

Jack and Teddy hurried over to Annie and the fallen bird. The bird was crouching, slightly spreading its wings. Its head was bowed as it made low, squeaking sounds. One of its tail feathers was bent.

"COO-COO!" Teddy said loudly. He looked at Jack. "I once journeyed to the Isle of Birds to study their language," he said. "I learned a bit of Dove, but no Raven."

"Don't worry," said Jack. "Annie talks to birds and animals in her own language."

"I'm sorry for what they did to you," Annie said softly to the raven. She stroked its silky black head. "What's your name?"

"ROK," the raven croaked.

"Rok? Your name is Rok?" said Annie.

"ROK! ROK!" croaked the raven.

"See, I told you," Jack said to Teddy.

"Rok, they were afraid of you for some reason," Annie said.

Rok made soft, bell-like sounds: "CRONG? CRONG?"

"Yes, that's why they knocked you out of the sky," said Annie. "One of your tail feathers is bent. But your wings don't seem hurt."

Rok fluttered his long black wings. He took a few feeble steps.

"Go on, Rok," Annie coaxed. "You can do it."

The raven flapped his wings again. "QUORK!" he croaked.

He lifted off the ground.

"Great!" said Annie, clapping.

Rok flapped his wings. He glided up into the twilight. He swooped with ease back down to Annie. "CAW! CAW!" he called, as if thanking her.

"Be careful, Rok!" Annie shouted.

They all waved as the raven sailed off into the sky.

Annie smiled at Jack and Teddy. "He was really nice," she said.

"Indeed he was," said Teddy. "I think your gentle words were healing to him."

"I wonder why the people here are so afraid of ravens," said Annie.

"Yeah," said Jack. "And what was that stuff about ghosts?"

"Ghosts?" said Teddy. He smiled. "You needn't fear ghosts if you're with me."

Jack shrugged. "I'm not really afraid," he said.

"Not afraid?" said a feeble voice.

Jack, Annie, and Teddy whirled around.

An old woman stood in the dark doorway of a cottage. She leaned forward. In a cracked voice, she said:

Where is the girl
who spins wool into thread?
Where are the boys
who play chess before bed?
Where is the hound
who waits to be fed?

The old woman stared at them with a fearful look in her eyes. Then she stepped back into her cottage and closed her door.

A shiver went up Jack's spine. "That was strange," he said.

"She must have been old Maggie, who worked at the castle," said Annie. "I wonder what she was talking about."

"I don't know," said Teddy. Then he grinned. "But she was good at rhyming, eh?"

Jack nodded. "Indeed she was," he said softly.

"Let's hurry along!" said Teddy. "Night comes fast upon us!"

Leaving the cottages behind, the three hurried on in the gathering dark. They left the village and followed the path through the woods.

Teddy held up his lantern to light their way. The wind blew the branches of the trees, making them whisper in the chilly autumn night.

When they finally came out of the woods, they all gasped in wonder.

"Oh, man," said Jack.

Towering before them in the moonlight were the walls of a huge stone castle.

CHAPTER FOUR

The Castle

The castle was still and silent. No candles burned in its windows. No guards stood at its gatehouse. No archers patrolled the tops of its walls.

"Hello!" Teddy shouted.

No one answered.

"Not very well protected, eh?" said Teddy. "Our mission should be easy."

"Yeah," said Annie.

Jack didn't say anything. He would have felt happier if guards *had* been protecting the castle. That would have seemed more normal.

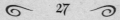

"Come along!" said Teddy.

Jack and Annie followed Teddy over a wooden bridge to the gatehouse.

Teddy held up his lantern before the arched double doors. Cobwebs sparkled in the misty light.

"Hello! May we enter?" he called.

Silence. They all stared at the heavy wooden doors.

"Never fear, I shall get us in," said Teddy.

The boy sorcerer put down his lantern. He took a deep breath. He rubbed his hands together. Then he stretched out his arms and shouted:

"*Open, ye two oaken doors. . . .*"

He looked at Jack and Annie. "Quick, what rhymes with *doors*?"

"Uh—floors?" said Jack.

"Good," said Teddy. He opened his arms again and yelled:

"*Open, ye two oaken doors!*
Or we will not mop up your floors!"

Nothing happened.

Teddy looked at Jack and Annie. "Bad rhyme," he said.

Annie frowned and nodded.

"Are you sure they're even locked?" said Jack.

"Let's see," said Annie. She pushed on one door. Jack pushed on the other.

Slowly the doors creaked open.

"Ah, brilliant!" said Teddy with a laugh. "Shall we?" He held out his hand and waved Jack and Annie through the open doorway.

The castle gatehouse was cold and empty. Jack could see his breath in the sharp air. He heard a creak. They all turned to look. The heavy doors moved by themselves and closed with a *thump*.

They all stared at the doors for a moment. Then Teddy broke the silence. "Interesting," he said cheerfully.

Jack tried to smile. "Indeed. Interesting," he said. He shivered. He couldn't tell if it was from cold or from fright. *Now?* he wondered. *Now are we entering the tunnel of fear?*

"Onward!" said Teddy. He led them through

the empty gatehouse onto the shadowy castle grounds.

There were no signs of life anywhere. Jack thought of the old woman's rhyme:

Where is the girl
who spins wool into thread?
Where are the boys
who play chess before bed?
Where is the hound
who waits to be fed?

Jack wondered what the rhyme could mean. *What girl? What boys? What hound?*

Teddy crossed the courtyard to the entrance of a large building. Jack and Annie quickly followed him.

Teddy held up his lantern so they could see inside. There were rows of clean, empty stalls. Saddles and bridles hung from pegs on the walls. Hay was piled in the corners.

"Must be the stables," said Jack.

"But no horses," said Annie.

"No matter, 'tis orderly," said Teddy. "Onward!"

He led them to the open doorway of another building. Teddy's lantern shone on a brick oven, a stone hearth, baskets of apples, and strings of onions hanging from the rafters.

"The kitchen," said Jack.

"But no cooks or servants," said Annie.

"No matter, 'tis orderly here, too," said Teddy. "Onward!"

As they wandered through the moonlit courtyard, Jack looked to his right and his left. He glanced behind them. *If there are ghosts*, he thought, *what do they look like? Halloween ghosts in sheets? See-through people like in the movies?*

He stopped. "Hey, guys!" he whispered loudly. "Wait a minute, wait a minute!"

"What is it?" said Annie.

Jack pushed his glasses into place. "Are we just going to keep wandering from building to building?" he said. "What's our strategy here?"

"Strategy?" asked Teddy.

"Jack means we should make a plan," said Annie.

"Ah, indeed," said Teddy. "Excellent idea. A plan, yes." He grinned. "How do we do that?"

"Well, first we ask ourselves: Where exactly are we going?" said Jack.

Teddy looked about. He pointed to a tower rising above the courtyard. "There," he said, "the keep. 'Tis where the family lives, the duke and duchess."

"Great," said Jack. "Now, what will we do when we get there?"

"Climb the stairs to each floor," said Teddy. "Have a look around."

"And if we see anything that's not orderly, we'll tidy it up!" said Annie.

"Excellent," said Teddy.

"And then?" asked Jack.

"We leave!" said Teddy. "Our mission done."

Jack nodded. This wasn't much of a plan—or

a mission, he thought. But he liked the "leaving" part. He hoped that happened before any ghosts showed up. "Okay," he said.

Holding his lantern to light their way, Teddy led them to the entrance of the castle keep. He pushed open a wooden door, and they all stepped inside.

Dark figures loomed against the stone walls.

"Ah!" Jack cried. He jumped back, bumping into Annie.

Annie laughed. "It's only our shadows," she said.

Jack felt silly. "Right. Sorry, sorry," he said. He took a deep breath. "Okay, let's find the stairway."

"Aye," said Teddy. He started walking slowly down a dark passageway. Jack and Annie followed close behind.

The air was heavy and damp. Jack's heart was pounding. *Now?* he wondered. *Now are we in the tunnel of fear?*

A moaning sound came through the passage-way. Then a loud *bang!*

"Yikes!" said Annie. She and Jack grabbed each other.

Teddy laughed. "'Twas only the shutters banging," he said.

"What about that moaning?" asked Jack.

"'Twas only the wind blowing through the crannies," said Teddy.

Jack took another deep breath and kept going. Soon they came to a twisting stairway.

"The stairs!" said Annie.

Good, thought Jack. Climbing the stairway was a solid part of their plan.

"Shall we?" said Teddy.

"Indeed. Upward!" said Jack, trying to sound like Teddy.

Teddy held up his lantern and started up the steep stone stairs. Jack and Annie followed. They climbed around and around the twisting stairway.

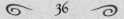

When they came to the first landing, Teddy led them to the doorway of a room. They peeked in. They saw rows of helmets, breastplates, gauntlets, shields, spears, and swords.

"The armor room," said Jack.

"Aye," said Teddy.

"Everything seems in order here," said Annie.

Jack nodded. He liked the order in the room. It made him feel safer.

"Shall we keep going?" said Teddy.

"Of course," said Jack. He was starting to feel a lot braver now.

They returned to the stairs and began climbing again. On the third floor, they peered through an arched entrance into a huge room.

Teddy used the candle from his lantern to light torches on either side of the doorway. In the flickering light, Jack saw a high ceiling and walls hung with tapestries.

"It's the great hall," he said, "where they have feasts and stuff."

"Let's look around," said Annie. "See if anything seems out of order."

As the three of them slowly walked forward, Jack kept an eye out for ghosts.

Teddy held up his lantern. It shone on a long banquet table.

"Aha!" he said. The table was littered with bread crumbs, candle wax, and the petals of dead flowers. The floor near the table was messy, too, with bits of food and meat bones.

"Finally we've found something to put in order," said Teddy. "Shall we?"

Jack caught sight of a straw broom in the corner. "Sure, I'll sweep," he said.

"I'll clear the table," said Annie.

"I will scrape the wax," said Teddy.

Jack grabbed the straw broom and began sweeping the floor around the table. He swept up apple peelings, fish bones, bits of eggshells, and old cheese.

As he swept everything into a neat pile, he

felt good. They were finally carrying out their mission. *We're bringing order to the castle, just like Merlin told us to,* he thought. *Soon we can leave.*

Suddenly Annie screamed.

Jack dropped his broom and whirled around.

"Look!" Annie cried, her eyes wide. She pointed toward a stone hearth at the other end of the great hall.

In front of the hearth, a large white bone hovered in the air. It bobbed up and down. Then it began floating straight toward them!

CHAPTER FIVE

Ghosts!

"AHHH!" yelled Teddy.

"AHHH!" yelled Jack.

"AHHH!" yelled Annie.

Still screaming, they all ran toward the door. The bone came after them.

Teddy led the way as they tore through the archway and scrambled up the winding staircase.

Jack looked behind them.

"It's still coming!" he shrieked.

"AHHH!" they all screamed again.

On the next landing, Teddy charged into a nearby room.

"Make haste!" he yelled.

He pulled Jack and Annie into the room and slammed the door behind them. Out of breath, they all leaned against the door, panting and trembling.

"Safe—" Teddy gasped. "Safe from the bone!" Then he started laughing.

Jack laughed, too. He laughed out of sheer terror. He couldn't stop.

"Listen, guys! Listen!" said Annie. "I hear a noise!"

Teddy stopped laughing. Jack clapped his hand over his mouth. He listened. He heard a faint clicking sound, but he couldn't see anything.

Teddy used the fire from his lantern to light torches near the door. Then they all looked about.

"Looks like a nursery," said Teddy.

The torchlight showed a kids' room. The room had three small beds. Wooden toys were scattered across the floor. A long white curtain fluttered from an open window.

The clicking noise seemed to be coming from a dark corner.

"What *is* that?" whispered Annie. She started toward the noise.

Jack and Teddy followed her. Teddy held up his lantern. His light shone on a child-sized spinning wheel. It sat in the corner near a basket of wool and a tall, dusty mirror.

The spinning wheel was spinning thread. But no one was touching it. *It was spinning all by itself.*

"Look!" whispered Annie.

She pointed to a low table near the spinning wheel. On the table was a chessboard. Large wooden chess pieces sat on the squares of the board.

But some of the pieces weren't just sitting!

As Jack, Annie, and Teddy watched, a horse piece slid slowly from one square to another. Then a queen piece did the same!

"Yikes!" said Annie.

"Ghosts!" said Teddy.

"Let's get out of here!" said Jack.

They bolted across the room. Teddy threw open the door. The white bone was hanging in the air, right outside the door!

"AHHH!" they all screamed.

Teddy slammed the door shut. They huddled together, afraid to leave and afraid to stay. Jack's heart was beating wildly. He couldn't breathe.

"I—I thought you weren't afraid of ghosts!" he said to Teddy, gasping.

"Yes, well, I believe I just discovered that I am!" said Teddy.

"What'll we do?" said Jack.

"A rhyme—a rhyme," said Teddy. He gave Annie his lantern. He threw out his arms and started a rhyme:

Spirits of the earth and air!

He looked at Jack and Annie. "Quick, what rhymes with *air*?"

"Bear!" said Jack.

Teddy shook his head. "I fear a bear might make things worse."

Jack tried hard to think of a better word to rhyme with *air*.

"Wait a minute!" said Annie. "I get it now! I get it!" She grinned at Jack and Teddy.

Has she lost her mind? Jack wondered.

"Remember what old Maggie said?" asked Annie. Then she recited:

"Where is the girl

who spins wool into thread?"

Annie pointed at the spinning wheel in the corner. "There she is!" she said. "She's spinning at that wheel."

Annie recited more:

"Where are the boys

who play chess before bed?"

Annie pointed at the chess table. "There they are!" she said. "They're probably her brothers! They're playing chess!"

She recited more:

"Where is the hound

who waits to be fed?"

Annie threw open the door to the nursery.

The bone was still hanging in the air. Jack and Teddy jumped back in fear.

"Don't be afraid!" said Annie. "It's just a dog—a hound! He's carrying a bone in his mouth. Don't you see? The girl, the boys, the hound—they're all here! They're just *invisible*!"

CHAPTER SIX

Merlin's Diamond

Jack and Teddy were speechless. They kept staring at Annie as she got down on her knees and talked to the invisible dog.

"Hi, you," she said in a soft voice. "Are you hungry?"

The bone dropped toward the floor. It flipped over, then rocked from side to side.

"See," Annie said to Jack and Teddy. "Now he's rolling on his back with his bone in his mouth. Poor thing."

"Poor thing?" said Jack.

"We have to help him," said Annie. She stood up. "We have to help *them*, too—the girl and her brothers."

She hurried across the room. Jack and Teddy followed. Annie stopped at the small spinning wheel.

"We can't see you," said Annie, "but we're not afraid of you. We want to help you. Can you hear me?"

The spinning wheel stopped spinning.

"She can hear us!" Annie said to Jack and Teddy. Annie turned back to the ghost girl. "What happened to you and your brothers and your dog and everyone else in the castle? How did you all become invisible?"

Jack felt a wave of cold air whoosh past him.

"I think she's moving," said Annie.

"Aye," said Teddy, "to the looking glass. See?"

An invisible finger had begun to write something in the thick dust of the mirror. Four words slowly appeared:

Diamond
of Destiny
stolen

"I can't believe it!" said Teddy. "This must be the secret castle that guards the Diamond of Destiny!"

"What's *that*?" said Jack.

"A magic diamond that belongs to Merlin," said Teddy. "It was set in the handle of the very sword King Arthur pulled from the stone many years ago."

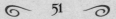

"Oh, I know that story," said Annie. "That's how Arthur became king!"

"Yes!" said Teddy. "And someday the Diamond of Destiny will give the same strength and power to the next rightful ruler of Camelot."

"That's what Merlin must have meant when he said the future of Camelot depends on us," said Annie.

"Indeed," said Teddy.

"Wait, wait," said Jack. "I'm confused. What does the Diamond of Destiny have to do with invisible kids and dogs?"

"After Arthur became king, Merlin gave the diamond to a noble family of Camelot," said Teddy. "The name of the family was kept secret. As long as the family kept the diamond safe, they would have good fortune. But should they fail to protect it, they would fade from life."

"Oh! So the family let the diamond get stolen," said Annie. "And now they've all turned into ghosts!"

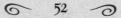

"Precisely," said Teddy.

"I wonder where the diamond was kept," said Jack.

"Good question," said Teddy. "Certainly some special hiding place, perhaps in one of the towers."

"Guys, look!" said Annie. She pointed to the wall near the mirror.

A long, heavy tapestry had been pulled aside to reveal a small door in the stone wall. The door was slowly swinging open.

"The ghost girl!" said Annie. "She's showing us the diamond's secret hiding place!"

The three of them hurried to the stone wall and looked inside a tiny cabinet. The walls of the cabinet were made of gold and ivory. But the cabinet was empty.

Annie looked around. "Ghost girl?" she said. "Who stole the Diamond of Destiny from its hiding place?"

Letters began to appear on the mirror again.

In the thick dust, the invisible finger wrote:

The Raven

"Oh, no," whispered Teddy. "Please, no."

Jack felt a fresh wave of fear. "Oh-no-please-no-*what*?" he said.

"Wait," said Teddy, pointing at the mirror.

The finger wrote one more word in the dust:

King

"Just as I feared," said Teddy in a hushed voice. "The Raven King!"

CHAPTER SEVEN

One, Two, Three!

"So that's why Merlin sent for those books!" said Teddy.

"What books? Who's the Raven King?" said Jack.

"Now it all makes sense," said Teddy.

"Who's the Raven King?" said Jack.

"But I wonder how he found the Diamond of Destiny," said Teddy.

"Teddy, who's the Raven King?" Jack nearly shouted.

"He's a terrifying creature who comes from

the Otherworld," said Teddy. "I read all about him in one of the books I brought Merlin from Morgan's library. As a boy, the Raven King longed to be a bird so he could fly. He stole a spell from the Wizard of Winter, but he didn't have the magic to make it work properly. So the spell only worked halfway. It made him half bird and half human."

"Oh, man," said Jack.

"Now he commands a huge army of ravens who treat him as their king," said Teddy.

"Why would he steal the Diamond of Destiny?" asked Annie.

"I don't know," said Teddy, "but we must get it back! For the sake of Camelot's future!"

"And for these ghost kids, too," said Annie, "and the ghost dog!"

She looked around the room. "Don't worry!" she called. "We'll help all of you! We'll get the Diamond of Destiny back!"

"We will?" asked Jack. "How? We don't know

where this crazy raven man lives or anything."

"Look! More writing," whispered Teddy. "She heard you."

Three more words slowly appeared in the mirror dust:

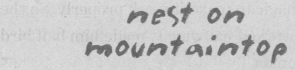

Jack felt cold air whoosh by him again. The curtain covering the window moved aside. A patch of moonlight shone on the floor.

Jack, Annie, and Teddy walked to the window and looked out. In the distance, a craggy mountain rose into the moonlit sky.

"Ah!" whispered Teddy. "So *there* dwells the Raven King! I had thought his nest was in the Otherworld."

"It might as well be," said Jack. "We'll never be able to get to the top of that mountain."

"Aye," said Teddy, "no mere mortal can climb that steep rock."

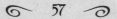

"How will we get the diamond back?" cried Annie.

"I said *no mere mortal*," said Teddy. "*I* am more than a mortal, remember? I'm a sorcerer."

"Yeah, but your rhymes never work," said Annie.

"True, but I have more than just rhymes," said Teddy. He pulled a twig out of his pocket. "See?"

"What's that?" said Jack.

"'Tis an enchanted hazel twig," said Teddy. "Its magic is strong enough to change me into anything I want."

"Oh, wow," said Annie.

"Did Morgan give you that?" asked Jack.

"No," said Teddy. "Morgan and Merlin do not even know I have it. A forest sprite, a cousin of my mother's, gave it to me, in case I was ever in urgent need."

"So what do you want to change into?" asked Annie.

"Why, a raven, of course!" Teddy said.

Teddy's crazy, thought Jack.

But Annie didn't seem to think so. "What a cool idea," she said.

They're both crazy, thought Jack.

"'Tis cool indeed," said Teddy. He held up the twig.

"Wait a minute!" said Jack. "Do you have a plan? I mean, what're you going to do once you change into a raven?"

"I shall fly up to the mountain nest," said Teddy. "Find the diamond. Bring it back. Mission done."

"And what do *we* do?" asked Annie.

"Wait here for me. I'll be back as soon as I can," said Teddy. He climbed up onto the window ledge. His moon shadow stretched across the floor.

"Good luck!" said Annie.

"Thank you!" said Teddy. He raised his hazel twig.

"Stop!" said Jack. "Can we discuss your 'plan' a little more?"

But Teddy was already sweeping his hazel twig through the air. He waved it from the top of his head to the tips of his toes.

"Teddy, stop!" said Jack.

But Teddy started his rhyme:

"O hazel twig from hazel tree!
Make me a raven—"

"Quick," he said, "a word that rhymes with *tree*?"

"Wait!" said Jack.

"Doesn't rhyme with *tree*," said Teddy.

"Three!" said Annie.

"Brilliant!" said Teddy. He started again:

"O hazel twig from hazel tree!
Make me a raven one, two, three!"

He waved the twig wildly.

"Careful!" said Jack. He ducked and covered his head.

Suddenly he heard a roar. He felt a blast of

heat. Then he heard a strange screech.

Jack looked up. Teddy's hazel twig had fallen to the floor. Jack saw Teddy's shadow on the floor, too. But it was no longer the shadow of a boy.

A chill went through Jack.

A large raven was perched on the window-sill. Moonlight shone on its sleek blue-black wings, its shaggy throat feathers, its thick neck and big beak.

A second raven stood beneath the window. It looked like the first, only smaller.

Where's Annie? Jack wondered wildly. He tried calling her name. But a terrible croak came from the back of his throat: "AWK-NEE!"

Jack felt as if he were caught in a terrible nightmare. With jerky turns of his head, he peered down at his own body.

His arms had turned into jet-black wings. His legs were spindly twigs that ended in four long, skinny toes with curved claws.

Teddy had accidentally changed them *all* into ravens. *One, two, three.*

CHAPTER EIGHT

SPREE! SPREE!

"CRA-JAH! CRA-AWK-NEE!" Teddy croaked.

Teddy was speaking Raven now, but Jack understood him perfectly. Teddy had said, *Sorry, Jack and Annie!*

Annie stepped forward. She fluttered to the window ledge and perched with Teddy.

"GRA-QUORK!" she croaked. *That's okay! This is fun!*

"QUORK?" Jack squeaked. *Fun?*

"GRO-JAH!" croaked Annie. "KAH-SPREE!" *Come on, Jack! Let's fly!*

Annie and Teddy lifted off the ledge and disappeared into the moonlit mist.

This can't be real, thought Jack. *It can't be real!*

He looked at his feathers and claws. He stretched out his right wing, then his left. He flapped them both. Before he knew what was happening, he lifted clumsily off the floor and landed on the window ledge.

Jack saw Annie and Teddy flying around in the moonlight. They were zipping about like acrobats—diving and tumbling through the air.

"AWK-NEE CAW!" Jack croaked. *Annie, come back!*

"SPREE! SPREE!" she called. *Fly! Fly!*

"AWK-NEE!"

Annie rose from a dive. In one easy swoop, she glided up and sat beside Jack on the window ledge.

This is so much fun, Jack! she croaked. *Don't just sit here!*

Teddy flew by them. *I'm off to the mountain-top!* he croaked. *Fly with me!*

Come on, Jack! croaked Annie. She took off after Teddy, swooping through the cool night air.

Oh, man! Fear clutched Jack's small raven heart. *I have definitely entered the tunnel of fear now,* he thought. Merlin's words echoed in his mind: *"Proceed onward with courage, and you will come out into the light."*

Jack looked out at the night. He closed his eyes. He jumped off the ledge.

Jack was falling! He opened his eyes and flapped. His wings lifted him up. He steadied himself. He hovered in the cold night air, his eyes darting from right to left. He looked down. He nearly fainted! The castle courtyard was far below!

Jack flapped wildly. He glided. He flapped again. He glided. Flapping and gliding, he climbed higher and higher into the sky.

Finally Jack caught up with Annie and

Teddy. They were circling in the air, waiting for him.

"RARK!" Jack croaked. *Onward!*

The three of them flew together through the moonlit night, heading for the nest of the Raven King. Except for the swooshing of their wings, they made no noise.

They soared up the side of the mountain, past hemlocks and tall pines. They flew through long, misty clouds.

As they glided toward the mountain's peak, Teddy let out a low croak: *Raven troops!*

Jack peered through the night. He couldn't believe his eyes. In the white moonlight, he saw *thousands* of ravens roosting on rocky ledges!

Jack, Annie, and Teddy kept flying. They soared above the troops, higher and higher, toward the craggy peak of the mountain. When they reached the top, Teddy let out a squawk.

There it is! he croaked. *The nest of the Raven King!*

CHAPTER NINE

A Piece of a Star

Teddy dropped down to a ledge. Jack and Annie followed. Hidden in the shadows, they crouched together, their dark feathers touching. They peered out at the moonlit lair of the Raven King.

The king's giant nest was tucked under a rocky overhang. It was made of mud, twigs, and long strips of tree bark. Two raven sentries were guarding its dark entrance.

Okay, Jack softly croaked, *what's the plan?*

Listen carefully, Teddy answered. In tiny *queeks* and *caws* of raven whispers, he spelled out a plan: *I'll distract the guards. Annie, you keep watch at the entrance. Jack, you go into the nest and get the diamond. Then both of you head back to the castle and wait for me there.*

What about the Raven King? croaked Jack.

I sense he's not here, croaked Teddy. *I see no legions of bodyguards. But we should hurry before he returns.*

Jack had lots more questions about the plan. But before he could ask them, Teddy lifted off his perch and flew toward the entrance.

Let's go! cried Annie, rising into the air.

Jack was in a panic. He fluffed out his feathers and croaked, *Wait, you guys!*

But it was too late! Teddy was already dive-bombing the raven sentries!

"ARK-ARK-ARK!"

The two sentries left their watch and flew at Teddy with short shrieks. They chased him high into the sky.

Annie zipped to the entrance of the nest. *Come on, Jack!* she croaked.

Jack jumped off the ledge and flew on to the giant nest. Without thinking, he stepped through the entrance.

He jerked his head from side to side. With his raven sight, he saw walls packed with dried mud, animal fur, vines, and sticks. The floor was covered with moss.

Jack took a few steps forward. He stopped. He saw no sign of the Raven King. He cocked his head from side to side, listening. All was quiet.

Jack looked around the nest. One part of the nest's wall looked different. It was black and shiny. He stepped toward it. He touched it with his beak. It wasn't a wall at all. It was a curtain of feathers.

Jack pushed through the feather curtain. Moonlight shone into the space behind it. Heaps of gold and silver coins glittered in the cool light. Pale pearls, emeralds, and rubies shone and sparkled.

Amid all the treasure was a blue-white crystal. It was no bigger than a marble. But it shone with a light all its own, like a piece of a star.

Jack knew at once the stone was the Diamond of Destiny. His raven heart thumping, he walked to the diamond and nudged it with his beak. As the diamond tilted, it shot forth beams of brilliant light.

"JAH! JAH!" Annie was calling to him from outside. "CREE-GRO!" *They're coming!*

Jack carefully picked up the diamond with his beak. He felt a surge of strength and courage.

Annie called another warning. But Jack wasn't afraid at all. He calmly walked out of the Raven King's nest back into the night.

More sentries had been alerted. They were flying toward the mountaintop, cawing madly in alarm.

"KRAK! KRAK! KRAK!"

Jack saw Annie perched on the ledge. *Hurry, Jack! Hurry!* she croaked.

Annie flew off the mountain. Holding the diamond in his beak, Jack gracefully flapped his wings and lifted into the air after her.

As he and Annie sailed down from the mountaintop, a chorus of *KRAK*s split the night. Thousands of roosting ravens rose into the sky like a giant black cloud. Their beating wings rumbled like thunder.

The cloud of ravens covered the light of the moon. The night was completely black.

"SPREE! SPREE!" Annie croaked. *Fly! Fly!*

She and Jack glided down through the dark

sky toward the duke's castle. The wing beats of the raven army still thundered above the mountaintop. But none of the ravens were chasing them.

They don't know what to do without their king, Jack thought. He wondered where their king was. But with the Diamond of Destiny in his beak, he felt no fear.

The farther Jack and Annie flew from the mountain, the more distant became the sound of the raven soldiers' wings.

The duke's castle came into sight. Jack saw the light of Teddy's lantern in the nursery. But he didn't want to stop flying just yet. Instead, he swooped over the castle keep, over the courtyard, the gatehouse, and the bridge, over the candlelit cottages and oak forest. Annie flew with him.

Finally they both glided smoothly back to the castle and landed on the window ledge of the nursery. The Diamond of Destiny was safe!

CHAPTER TEN

Where Is It?

Jack and Annie perched on the ledge and peered into the nursery. Teddy's lantern and hazel twig were still on the floor. But there was no sign of Teddy.

Teddy's not here yet, croaked Annie. *Let's go ahead and put the diamond back in its place.*

Jack didn't move. He didn't want to give up the diamond quite yet. It still made him feel incredibly brave.

Jack? croaked Annie. *Let's put it back in its hiding place. I'll move the tapestry.*

Annie flapped to the long tapestry hanging on the wall. Fluttering in the air, she took its edge in her beak. She tried to pull it aside, but it was too heavy. She let go.

I can't move it, she croaked, *not as long as I'm a raven. I guess we'll have to wait for Teddy to change us back into ourselves.*

She flapped to the window ledge and landed beside Jack. Jack was relieved. The longer he could hold on to the diamond, the better.

Hey! croaked Annie. *Maybe we could use Teddy's magic hazel twig ourselves! I can come up with better rhymes than him anyway. It won't hurt to try.*

Jack shook his head. But Annie didn't notice. She hopped down to the hazel twig under the window. She carefully picked it up with her beak.

She fluttered back up to the ledge beside Jack. Then she moved her head from side to side, passing the twig over Jack's feathered head, his body, his wings, and his claws. The twig passed over her feathery body and wings as well.

With the twig still in her beak, she made a deep croaking sound.

"HA-HA-REE-REE!
JAH-JAH-AWK-NEE!"
O hazel twig from hazel tree!
Make him Jack, and make me, me!

There was a mighty roar and a flash of light and a blast of heat!

Then Jack heard Annie giggle. "Yippee! I made the magic work for us. Look."

Jack looked down at his arms and legs and feet. "Ohh, man," he breathed.

Awk-nee and Jah were gone. Annie and Jack were back.

Jack wiggled his fingers and toes. He felt his face: his mouth, his nose, his ears. He loved having his own body back!

"Teddy's going to be so surprised," said Annie.

"He acts like he's the only kid who can do magic." She looked around the nursery. "Hi! We're back!" she called to the invisible children. "Guess what? We've got the diamond!"

"The diamond! Where is it?" said Jack. "I must've dropped it when you changed us!"

Suddenly they heard a swoosh and a flapping at the window.

"Teddy!" cried Annie. She and Jack whirled around.

But Teddy wasn't there.

Instead, perched on the ledge of the nursery window was a horrifying creature. He was part human and part raven. He had silky feathers for hair, a beak for a nose, sharp claws, and a billowing feathered cape that glistened in the moonlight like shiny black armor.

"Good evening," said the Raven King.

CHAPTER ELEVEN

Or Else!

Jack and Annie were too stunned to speak.

Staring at the bizarre creature, Jack remembered the story of the Raven King—how the king had wanted to be a bird, how he had stolen a spell from the Wizard of Winter, how the spell had worked only halfway and left him half bird and half human.

The Raven King jumped from the window to the floor. One by one, his raven bodyguards swooshed into the room after him. At least twenty ravens came through the window. Soon

Jack and Annie were surrounded by dark wings, sharp beaks, and bright eyes.

Once his guards were in place, the Raven King twisted his head from side to side, looking from Jack to Annie. "Where are the two ravens who stole my diamond?" he asked in a raspy voice.

"What diamond?" asked Annie.

"What . . . what ravens?" asked Jack, his voice trembling. He wished desperately that he still had the Diamond of Destiny to give him strength and courage.

"The ravens that came to this castle after raiding my treasure room," said the Raven King. "Where are they hiding?"

Jack tried to imagine that he *was* still holding the diamond. "We don't know anything about them," he said in a low, steady voice. Pretending to hold the diamond actually made him feel brave.

"You don't know anything about them?" said the Raven King.

"No," said Jack. "You must have the wrong castle."

"Ah, the wrong castle," said the Raven King.

"Yes," said Jack.

"Perhaps you're right," said the Raven King. "But are you certain you haven't seen them? They look very much like this little one here."

The Raven King threw his cape over his shoulder and held up an iron birdcage. A raven was held captive inside.

"JAH, AWK-NEE!" the raven croaked.

"Teddy!" cried Annie.

"His name is Teddy?" said the Raven King. "How charming. I've caught a Teddy. I think he'll make a wonderful pet, don't you?"

Jack was horrified to see Teddy trapped in the Raven King's cage. "It's not charming," he said. "It's cruel. You better let him go, or else!"

"Yeah, let him go," said Annie. "Or else."

"Or else?" said the Raven King. "Or else what?" With backward jerks of his head, he laughed a raspy laugh.

As the king laughed, Jack glanced at the floor under the window. He saw the hazel twig. He moved toward it.

The Raven King caught sight of him. His laugh stopped abruptly. "CREE! CAW!" he croaked to one of his bodyguards.

Jack dashed for the twig. But before he could grab it, the king's bodyguard had swooped across the floor and picked up the twig in his beak. As the raven carried it to the top of the window, Jack noticed that one of his tail feathers was bent.

"Jack, look, it's Rok!" said Annie. She called up to the bird. "Rok! Rok!"

From his perch above the window, the raven looked down at Annie.

"Rok, it's me, Annie," she said. "I helped you when the people in the village threw stones at you. Remember?"

"What nonsense," croaked the Raven King. "Bring me the stick, bird."

Rok didn't move. Gripping the hazel twig in his beak, he stared down at Annie.

"Give the twig to Jack, Rok," she said. "So he can turn Teddy back into a boy."

"So that ugly little stick is a magic wand, is it?" said the Raven King. "Bring it to me, bird. Now!"

"Don't do it, Rok," said Annie. "Don't let him boss you around anymore."

The raven stared at Annie for a moment

with his dark brown eyes. He looked at the Raven King. He looked back at Annie. Then he swooped down to Jack and dropped the hazel twig at his feet.

Jack grabbed it.

"Traitor!" the Raven King shrieked at Rok. "You'll pay for this!" He lunged toward the raven. Rok tried to escape, but the king grabbed him by the throat.

Jack had to save Rok! He pointed the twig at the Raven King's back and shouted:

"O hazel twig from hazel tree!
Make him what he wanted to be!"

A deafening wind roared through the room. A blinding light flashed. Then all was clear.

The Raven King had vanished. His cape lay on the floor. Rok hopped away, unharmed.

From under the feathered cape came a hoarse cry. *Awk.*

Annie lifted the cape and uncovered a tiny raven. "Ohh!" she said softly.

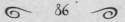

The bird stretched out his scrawny neck. *Awk*, he croaked again.

"Hello yourself," Annie said, smiling. She stroked the downy feathers on the creature's head. Then she looked up at Jack. "How did you come up with that rhyme?"

"It just came to me," said Jack.

"I knew I had to save Rok. But I didn't want to hurt the Raven King. I think I actually felt sorry for him."

"So you helped him finally get what he wanted," said Annie. "You turned him into a baby raven."

"Yeah," Jack said. "Now he can live his whole life as a bird."

Rok flew up to the window ledge. He looked around at the other ravens. It was clear he had become their new leader.

"GRO! GRO!" Rok croaked.

He stepped aside. The raven troops began to leave the nursery, one by one. Two of them

escorted the new member of their flock as he timidly flapped his small wings.

Rok was the last to leave. He stared at Annie and Jack with a long gaze. Then he lifted off the window ledge and flew away into the light of the silver dawn.

CHAPTER TWELVE

A New Day

Queek.

A little croak came from the cage on the floor.

"Teddy!" cried Annie.

"We almost forgot you!" said Jack.

Queek, Teddy croaked again.

"Let *me* change him back," Annie said to Jack.

"Okay, but let me get out of the way first," said Jack. He handed Annie the hazel twig. Then he quickly stepped over to the window.

Annie moved closer to Teddy's cage. She

closed her eyes and thought for a moment. Then she waved the wand over the cage and said:

"O hazel twig from hazel tree!
Make him Teddy! Set him free!"

There was a mighty roar, a blast of heat, and a blaze of light! Then the cage was gone, and Teddy was a boy again, sitting on the floor.

"Yay!" said Annie.

"Nicely done," said Teddy. "Thanks."

"Welcome back!" said Jack. He and Annie helped Teddy stand up.

Teddy shook his arms and legs. "Ahhh! 'Tis good to be human again!" he said. "And now we must help the duke's family. Where's the diamond?"

"We lost it!" said Annie.

"Yeah, I had it in my beak," said Jack. "But I must have dropped it when Annie changed us back into ourselves."

"Don't worry," said Teddy, "it must be here somewhere."

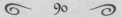

The three of them got on their hands and knees and started crawling around the floor of the nursery. There was no sign of the diamond. Suddenly Jack heard Teddy gasp.

"Oh, my," Teddy whispered. "Look." He was staring at the corner.

The Diamond of Destiny was rising from the basket of wool by the spinning wheel.

"The ghost girl must have hidden it when the Raven King came!" whispered Annie.

The diamond moved slowly toward Jack and stopped in front of him. Jack held out his hand, and the diamond settled into his palm.

"Thank you," Jack said to the ghost girl. "I'll put it back in its place now."

Carefully holding the diamond, Jack crossed the room. Annie pulled the tapestry aside, and Jack opened the golden door of the cabinet.

He looked one last time at the shining stone. "I really felt brave when I was carrying this diamond," he said softly.

"Jack," said Annie, "you were pretty brave just now without it."

"Indeed you were," said Teddy.

Jack smiled. He carefully put the Diamond of Destiny back in its place and closed the golden door. Then Annie covered the cabinet once more with the tapestry.

The air in the nursery grew warmer. A girl

began to take shape beside Teddy. She wore a white nightgown. She had dark curly hair. She was about Teddy's age.

At the chess table, two boys took shape, too. They looked just alike. They were twins about Annie's age.

At first the children were a bit pale and cloudy. Slowly they grew more and more visible, until they were solid and rosy-cheeked.

At the same time, a large brown dog became visible by the door. He barked and ran to the girl.

"Oliver!" she cried. She hugged him. Then she looked at Jack, Annie, and Teddy. She gave them a big smile. "Hello," she said.

"Hi!" said Annie. "Are the three of you the only people in this castle?"

"Oh, no, everyone else is here, too," the girl said, "but they were all asleep when the Raven King stole the diamond. We were supposed to be asleep, too. But sometimes we like to sneak out

of bed and play. We were playing hide-and-seek
when I found the secret door behind the tapestry. I wanted to see the diamond better, so I put
it on the window ledge to catch the moonlight.
Then Tom and Henry started to play chess—"
She pointed to the boys.

"Gwendolyn started spinning," said Tom. "And

Oliver went down to the great hall to look for scraps."

"That's when the Raven King swooped down

to the window and stole the diamond," said Gwendolyn. "Before we could even go tell our mother and father, we began to fade away."

"Mother! Father!" said Tom, as if he'd just remembered their parents. "We must wake them, Gwendolyn!"

"I know," she said. "We shall go upstairs and wake them at once. Since they were sleeping, I suspect they never even knew they were invisible!"

Gwendolyn took her brothers' hands, and the three of them started out of the nursery. At the door, she looked back at Jack, Annie, and Teddy. "Thank you for helping us," she said, "whoever you are."

The duke's children then slipped out of the nursery. Oliver grabbed his bone and bounded after them.

Jack handed the hazel twig to Teddy.

"Listen," Jack said. "I don't think this is something that kids should play with—even sorcerer kids. You'd better give it back to your cousin."

"Aye, perhaps that is a good plan," said Teddy. He grinned impishly as he slipped the twig back into his pocket. Then he gestured toward the door. "Shall we?"

Jack and Annie nodded.

Teddy picked up his lantern and blew out the candle. Then he led them all out of the castle nursery into the hallway. As they started down the stairs, servants rushed by.

"Ring the bells!" one said.

"Bring water for the duke and duchess!" said another.

"We're getting a late start today!" said a third.

Jack, Annie, and Teddy kept winding down the stairs, past the great hall, past the armor room, down to the entrance of the keep.

As they stepped into the courtyard, bright sunlight shone on the castle towers. The bells began to ring. Roosters crowed. Horses neighed.

Servants were making a big cooking fire. A blacksmith was pounding his anvil. A milkmaid was hauling her pails.

In the bright daylight, Jack, Annie, and

Teddy walked through the busy courtyard. They passed through the gatehouse and crossed the wooden bridge. When they got to the other side, they looked back.

Archers now stood guard on top of the castle walls.

Teddy waved to them. Then he looked at Jack and Annie. "Order has returned to the castle!" he said. "Our mission is done!"

Laughing, they ran through the patch of trees toward the small village. As they hurried along the dirt path past the cottages, they saw villagers in their doorways. They were all staring in the direction of the ringing castle bells.

Maggie, the old woman, grinned toothlessly at the three of them. "The bells are ringing again," she said in a creaky voice.

"Yes!" said Jack. "The boys and the girl and the hound are all back! There's nothing to be afraid of anymore. The whole castle is alive and well!"

Jack, Annie, and Teddy left the village and

headed for the woods. As they walked through the fallen leaves, sunlight filtered down through the tree branches.

Merlin's words echoed in Jack's mind: *You are about to enter a tunnel of fear. Proceed onward with courage, and you will come out into the light.*

Jack looked around. The forest was bright with the most beautiful golden light he had ever seen.

CHAPTER THIRTEEN

Jack and Annie's Magic

Jack, Annie, and Teddy crunched through fallen leaves until they came to Merlin's oak. They found the hidden door near the rope ladder. Teddy pushed on the bark.

The door opened. One by one, they slipped into the candlelit hollow of the tree trunk. Merlin was sitting in his tall wooden chair.

"So you restored order to the castle?" he said calmly.

"Yes, sir," said Teddy. "Had to use a bit of magic, but now all is well."

"Your rhyming must have improved," Merlin said to Teddy.

Teddy grinned sheepishly. "Well, to be truthful, the real magic was not in my rhymes. 'Twas the magic of Jack and Annie's courage and kindness that saved the day—and saved me, too."

"Indeed?" said Merlin.

"Aye," said Teddy. "They have a magic as powerful as any sorcerer's rhymes or enchanted hazel twig."

Merlin raised a bushy eyebrow. "Enchanted hazel twig?" he said.

"'Tis only a figure of speech," Teddy said quickly.

Merlin turned to Jack and Annie. "I thank you for your help," he said. "All the realm of Camelot thanks you."

"You're welcome," they said.

Merlin stood up. "Come along, my boy," he said to Teddy. "I will help speed you back to

Morgan now. My research is done. We must return these rare books to her library."

He reached down and picked up a stack of ancient-looking books from the floor. He piled them into Teddy's arms.

Teddy turned awkwardly with his books. Then he and Jack and Annie followed Merlin out of the heart of the oak.

The sun had risen higher in the sky. The woods were still.

Teddy peered over the tops of the books. "I suppose we must say good-bye now," he said to Jack and Annie.

"When will we see you again?" asked Annie.

"When duty calls, I suppose," said Teddy. He looked at Merlin.

The magician smiled.

"Will you be able to find your way home all right?" Teddy asked them.

"Oh, sure," said Jack. "The tree house will take us back."

He and Annie looked up at the magic tree house at the top of the oak. A sudden gust of wind rustled the leaves.

Jack and Annie turned back to Merlin and Teddy. But they were gone. Bright yellow leaves swirled and danced in the spot where they'd been standing.

"Wow . . . ," said Annie.

"Yeah . . . ," said Jack.

"Well," said Annie, sighing. "Onward?"

"*Home*ward!" said Jack.

Annie started up the rope ladder. Jack followed. When they climbed inside the tree house, Merlin's leaf invitation was fluttering off the floor. Before it could blow out the window, Annie grabbed it. She pointed to the words *Frog Creek*.

"I wish we could go there!" she said.

The wind started to blow.

The tree house started to spin.

It spun faster and faster!

Then everything was still.

Absolutely still.

* * *

Jack opened his eyes. He and Annie sat quietly on the floor of the tree house for a moment. Jack looked out the window. High overhead, a bird was soaring through the dusky sky.

Jack could hardly believe that just a little while ago, he had been a bird himself.

"Ready to go home?" said Annie.

Jack nodded. There was no way to explain what had just happened to them, he thought. There was no way to even talk about it.

Annie carefully placed Merlin's autumn leaf in the corner of the tree house, next to their Royal Christmas Invitation. Then she and Jack climbed down the ladder and started through the woods.

In the gathering dark of Halloween night, nothing seemed very spooky. Jack knew all the trees. He knew the familiar path out to their street.

As he and Annie headed toward home, three creatures stepped onto the sidewalk in front of them—a hideous witch, a grinning skeleton, and a huge, hairy eyeball.

The creatures cackled and rattled and hissed.

Jack and Annie laughed.

"Oh, brother," said Jack.

"Good costumes," said Annie.

Jack and Annie crossed their yard and climbed their front steps. "Are you ready for trick-or-treating?" said Annie.

Jack pushed his glasses into place. "You know, I think maybe I'll stay home this year," he said, "and help Mom and Dad give out the treats."

"Yeah, maybe I will, too," said Annie. "But I think I'll wear my vampire-princess costume anyway."

Jack smiled. "Cool," he said.

Then he and Annie slipped inside their warm, cozy house—and closed the door against the dark of All Hallows Eve.

A Note from the Author

Fairy tales and mythology often inspire ideas for my work. While I was writing *Haunted Castle on Hallows Eve*, details of old stories from Ireland, Wales, Scotland, England, and Persia found their way into my story. For example, in a book of Celtic tales from Ireland and Wales, I read many stories about people being transformed into animals. I also read about an army of ravens called the "raven troops." In a collection of stories from *The Arabian Nights*, I came across a magnificent bird called the Roc. All these legends stirred my imagination—and the

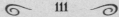

next thing I knew, I was writing a story in which my characters transformed into ravens and saved the life of an amazing bird named Rok.

When researching the ancient world of the British Isles, I learned that it was common for people to have awe and respect for sacred stones. I learned, in particular, about a famous stone in Scotland known as the "Stone of Destiny," which is surrounded by myth and legend. The stone was once used in sacred ceremonies for enthroning kings. This information inspired me to create Merlin's "Diamond of Destiny." And where did I get my idea for Teddy's magic hazel wand? For many years, I have loved a certain poem by the Irish poet William Butler Yeats. In the first stanza of "The Song of Wandering Aengus," Yeats writes:

I went out to the hazel wood,
Because a fire was in my head,

And cut and peeled a hazel wand,
And hooked a berry to a thread;
And when white moths were on the wing,
And moth-like stars were flickering out,
I dropped the berry in a stream
And caught a little silver trout.

Old tales and poetry from around the world are a constant source of inspiration for storytellers. Creating something new from something old allows us to link hands with people of the past. Or, as Morgan le Fay once said to Jack and Annie (in Magic Tree House #16, *Hour of the Olympics*), "The old stories are always with us. We are never alone."

Fun Activities for Jack and Annie and *You*!

Trick and Treat!

Why say trick *or* treat? You can have your trick and eat it too!

If you're feeling creative, there are many ways to make everyday snacks seem spooky. Wrap an unopened lollipop in a white napkin, draw on some eyes, and you have a ghost pop! Ask an adult to cut up some hot dogs, then spike them with toothpicks and dip them in ketchup to make "finger" food.

Or follow the recipe below to make delicious deviled eggs . . . that look just like eyeballs!

Deviled Eggs
You will need:

- 6 eggs
- A pot of water
- 1/8 teaspoon of salt, plus an extra pinch
- 2 tablespoons of mayonnaise
- 1/2 teaspoon of dry mustard
- 1/4 teaspoon of pepper
- Blue food coloring

- 12 slices of black olives
- A few pinches of paprika (optional)
- A fork and a knife
- A bowl and a plate
- An adult to help you

1. Put your eggs in the pot of water. Add a pinch of salt.

2. Ask your adult helper to bring the water to a boil. After 12 minutes, your helper should pour out the water.

3. Let the eggs cool for 20 minutes. Then peel off the shells. Throw the shells away, but keep the boiled eggs on a plate.

4. Have your helper cut each egg in half lengthwise.

5. Put all of the yolks into a bowl. Add mayonnaise, dry mustard, the 1/8 teaspoon of salt, pepper, and a few drops of food coloring.

6. Mash the mixture together with a fork.

7. Place scoops of the mixture back inside the egg whites. Use up all of the mixture.

8. Place a slice of black olive on top of each egg. The olive is the pupil, and the yolk mixture is the iris.

9. If you want to add some redness to your egg eyes, sprinkle just a bit of paprika onto the whites.

10. Cover the plate of eggs with plastic wrap. Put the plate in the refrigerator for at least an hour. Then dare your friends and family to take a bite!

Puzzle of the Haunted Castle

Jack and Annie learned many new things on their Hallows Eve adventure. Did you?

Put your knowledge to the test with this puzzle. You can use a notebook or make a copy of this page if you don't want to write in your book.

1. The invisible boys play this game.

☐ ○ ☐ ☐ ☐

2. Teddy's magic wand is a twig from this type of tree.

☐ ☐ ☐ ○ ☐

3. This raven helps Jack and Annie defeat the Raven King.

○ ☐ ☐

4. Merlin's invitation to Jack and Annie is written on one of these.

○ ☐ ☐ ☐

5. The Raven King steals the Diamond of

_____.

□ □ □ ○ □ □ □

6. Jack and Annie find Merlin in this type of tree.

○ □ □

7. The invisible dog holds this in its mouth.

□ ○ □ □

8. A large dark-colored bird.

○ □ □ □ □

9. A duchess's husband is called this.

○ □ □ □

10. The Raven King once stole a spell from the Wizard of _____ .

○ □ □ □ □ □

Now look at your answers above. The letters that are circled spell a word—but that word is scrambled! Can you unscramble it to spell the mythical place where Teddy's mother comes from?

Track the facts with Jack and Annie!

Magic Tree House® Fact Trackers are the must-have, all-true companions to your favorite Magic Tree House® adventures!

Here's a special preview of

Magic Tree House®
MERLIN MISSIONS #3
SUMMER OF THE SEA SERPENT

For Jack and Annie, summer is a time
for swimming, sunshine . . . and snakes!

Available now!

Excerpt copyright © 2004 by Mary Pope Osborne.
Illustrations copyright © 2004 by Sal Murdocca. Published by Random House
Children's Books, a division of Penguin Random House LLC, New York.

CHAPTER ONE

Summer Solstice

Jack was sitting on the porch reading the newspaper. It was a warm summer day, but the porch was shady and cool.

Annie poked her head out of the screen door. "Hey, Mom says she'll drive us to the lake this afternoon," she said.

Jack didn't raise his eyes from the weather page. "Did you know today is the summer solstice?" he said.

"What's that?" asked Annie.

"It's the official first day of summer," said

Jack. "There's more daylight today than on any other day of the year."

"Cool," said Annie.

"Starting tomorrow, the days will get shorter and shorter," said Jack.

A loud screech came from overhead.

"Look," said Annie, "a seagull!"

Jack looked up. A large white gull was circling in the bright noon sky. "What's he doing here?" asked Jack. "The ocean's two hours away."

The gull swooped down and screeched again.

"Maybe he's a messenger from Morgan or Merlin," said Annie. "Maybe one of them sent him to tell us the tree house is finally back."

Jack's heart began to pound. He put down the newspaper. "You think so?" he asked.

Jack and Annie hadn't seen the magic tree house since their Merlin Mission to a haunted castle last Halloween. Jack had begun to worry that the tree house might never come back.

"Look, he's flying toward the woods," said Annie.

Jack jumped up. "Okay," he said. "Let's go."

"We'll be back soon, Mom!" Annie called. Then she and Jack dashed across their yard. They ran down their street and into the Frog Creek woods.

The shady woods were dappled with sunlight. The air smelled fresh and clean. Jack and Annie hurried past the leafy trees, until they came to the tallest oak. High in the oak branches, the magic tree house was waiting for them.

"Wow," Jack and Annie said together. The tree house looked exactly the same as when they'd last seen it.

Annie grabbed the rope ladder and started up. Jack followed. When they climbed inside the tree house, no one was there.

"Look, our Royal Invitation is still here," said Annie. She picked up the card that had taken them to Camelot on Christmas Eve.

"And our leaf from Merlin is still here," said Jack. He picked up the yellow autumn leaf that had sent them on their Halloween mission.

"This is new," said Annie. She picked up a pale blue seashell. The shell was shaped like a small fan. There was writing on it.

"Hey, this looks like Merlin's handwriting!" said Annie. "We must be going on another mission for Merlin!" She read aloud the message from the magician:

To Jack and Annie of Frog Creek:
On this summer solstice, journey to
a land lost in mist, to a time even
before Camelot. Follow my rhyme
to complete your mission.

—M.

Annie looked up. "What rhyme?" she said.

"Let me see." Jack took the shell from her and turned it over. On the other side was a poem. Jack read the poem aloud:

Before night falls on this long summer day,
A shining sword must find its way
Into your hands and out of the gloom—
Or Camelot's king shall meet his doom.
To begin your quest for this Sword of Light,
Call for the help of the Water Knight.
Then pass through the Cave of the Spider Queen—

"Spider Queen?" Annie interrupted. She frowned. Spiders were about the only thing she was afraid of.

"Don't think about it now," said Jack. "Let's keep going." He read on:

. . . pass through the Cave of the Spider Queen
And swim with a selkie clothed in green.
Enter the Cove of the Stormy Coast,
Dive 'neath the Cloak of the Old Gray Ghost—

Jack stopped reading. "Old Gray Ghost?" he said.

"Don't think about it now," said Annie. "Keep going."

Jack read more:

Answer a question with love, not fear.

With rhyme and sword, your home is near.

Both Jack and Annie were silent for a moment. "That's a lot to do before nightfall," Jack finally said.

"Yeah," said Annie, "and I'm a little worried about the spider part."

"And the ghost part," said Jack.

"Hey," said Annie, "if we're going on another Merlin Mission, I'll bet Teddy will come with us! He can help us get through the scary parts."

"Right," said Jack. Just hearing Teddy's name made him feel braver.

"So," said Annie. "Onward?" *Onward* was Teddy's favorite word.

"Onward!" said Jack. He pointed to the handwriting on the pale blue shell. "I wish we could go to the time before Camelot!"

The wind started to blow.

The tree house started to spin.

It spun faster and faster.

Then everything was still.

Absolutely still.

Magic Tree House®

Magic Tree House® Merlin Missions

Magic Tree House®
Super Edition

#1: WORLD AT WAR, 1944

Magic Tree House®
Fact Trackers

More Magic Tree House®

CALLING ALL ADVENTURERS!

Join the

MAGIC TREE HOUSE®
KIDS' ADVENTURE CLUB

Members receive:

- Exclusive packages delivered throughout the year

- Members-only swag

- A sneak peek at upcoming books

- Access to printables, games, giveaways, and more!

With a parent's help, visit MagicTreeHouse.com to learn more and to sign up!

RHCB MagicTreeHouse.com

BRING MAGIC TREE HOUSE TO YOUR SCHOOL!

Magic Tree House musicals now available for performance by young people!

Ask your teacher or director to contact Music Theatre International for more information:
BroadwayJr.com
Licensing@MTIshows.com
(212) 541-4684

MAGIC TREE HOUSE COLLECTION

DINOSAURS BEFORE DARK KIDS

MAGIC TREE HOUSE COLLECTION

The Knight at Dawn KIDS

ATTENTION, TEACHERS!

Mary Pope Osborne's
Classroom Adventures Program

The Magic Tree House **CLASSROOM ADVENTURES PROGRAM** is a free, comprehensive set of online educational resources for teachers developed by Mary Pope Osborne as a gift to teachers, to thank them for their enthusiastic support of the series. Educators can learn more at MTHClassroomAdventures.org.

MAGIC TREE HOUSE®